THE BIG BOOK OF
SUPERMAN™

by Noah Smith

*Superman created by
Jerry Siegel and Joe Shuster.
By special arrangement with
the Jerry Siegel family.*

downtown bookworks

downtown bookworks

Downtown Bookworks Inc.
265 Canal Street
New York, New York 10013
www.downtownbookworks.com

Designed by Georgia Rucker
Typeset in Geometric and CCHeroSandwich

Printed in China
July 2017

ISBN 978-1-941367-45-2

10 9 8 7 6 5 4 3 2 1

Look! A streak of blue and red in the sky! A mighty figure hoists a car above his head and bounces bullets off his chest like they are Ping-Pong balls! It can only be Superman! But who *is* Superman?

THE ADVENTURES BEGIN

Many years ago, the planet Krypton orbited a distant red sun. It was a peaceful world of technological wonders. But one brilliant scientist, Jor-El, discovered that Krypton was doomed to explode.

Jor-El and his wife, Lara, raced to build a rocket that could safely carry their baby, Kal-El, to another world. Tearfully, Kal-El's parents blasted him into space, just as Krypton's destruction began.

Kal-El, the last son of Krypton, sped through the stars toward Earth—the planet Jor-El and Lara had chosen to be his new home.

MEET THE KENTS

The rocket crashed to Earth outside the town of Smallville. Jonathan and Martha Kent, owners of a nearby farm, found the smoking wreckage. And, to their shock, there was a baby inside!

THUD!

The Kents knew this baby from space needed a family. They adopted him and named him Clark. Martha and Jonathan taught Clark to work hard and be kind.

From the Kents, Clark learned that money and power don't make you a good person. What makes you a good person is the way you treat others.

A BOY LIKE NO OTHER

s Clark grew older, the Earth's yellow sun supercharged his Kryptonian body. He began to exhibit astonishing new powers.

He lifted up a heavy crib with one tiny toddler hand.

He used his heat vision to slice through unbreakable thread!

SNAP!

The Kents told Clark to keep his powers secret until he could learn to control them. So he practiced and practiced. When he was ready, he could use those powers to help people all over the world.

He squeezed a piece of coal so hard it turned into a diamond!

A HERO IS HERE!

As an adult, Clark moved to the big city—Metropolis—and began working at a newspaper.

Soon the streets buzzed with stories about a brave new champion who was here to help. They called him the Man of Steel.

GOOD GRIEF! EVERY BUILDING ON THE TOWN SQUARE IS TOPPLING! IN ONE MORE SECOND THEY'LL COLLAPSE COMPLETELY!

When criminals ran amok, when disaster struck, or when anyone was in danger, Clark knew. . .

And off he would soar—up, up, and away.

THE DAILY PLANET

Clark Kent is quiet and gentle, but he's also one of the world's greatest reporters. No one suspects the secret identity he's hiding behind those glasses. Whenever there's excitement, he slips away. That's why he's never there when Superman arrives, right?

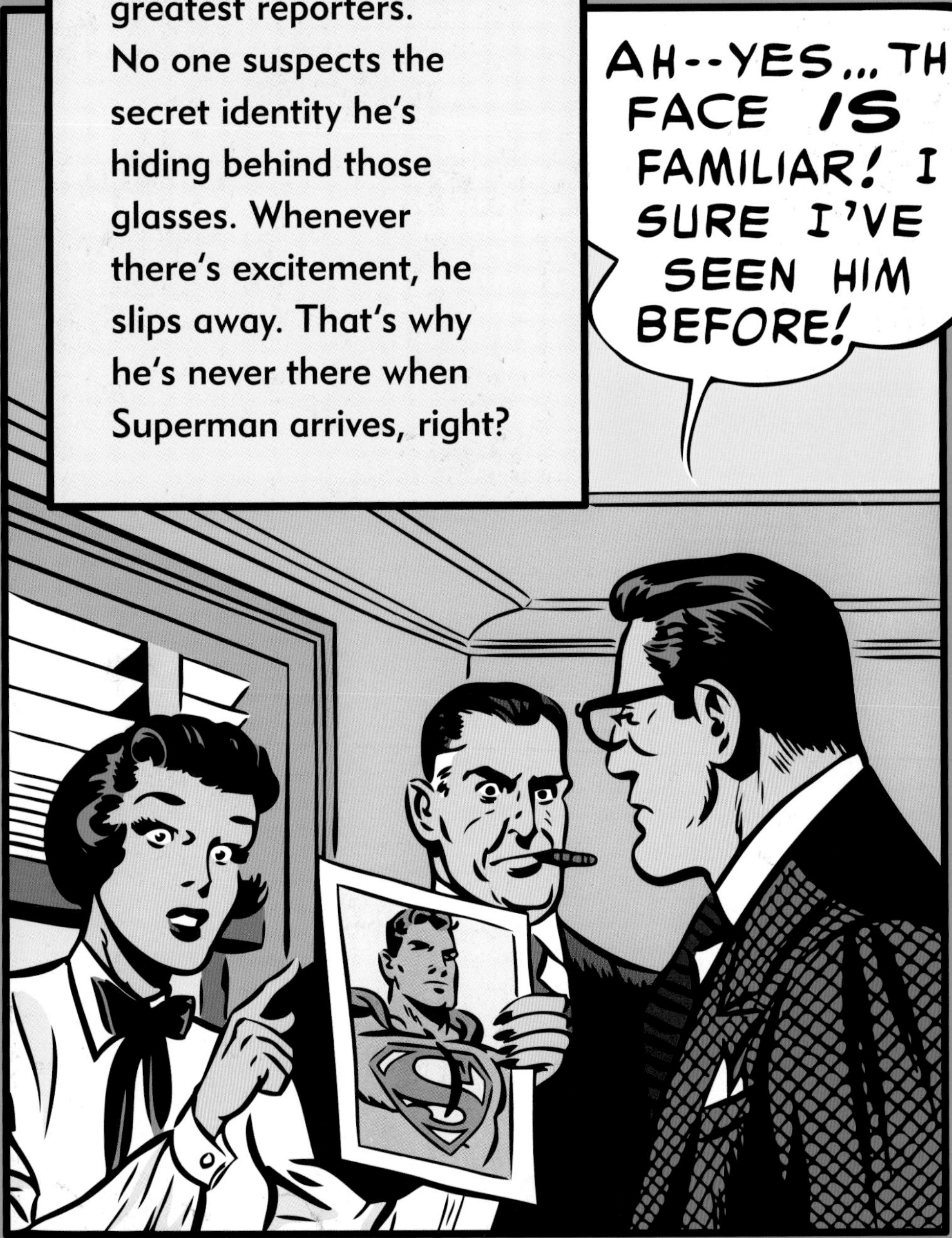
AH--YES... THE FACE *IS* FAMILIAR! I'M SURE I'VE SEEN HIM BEFORE!

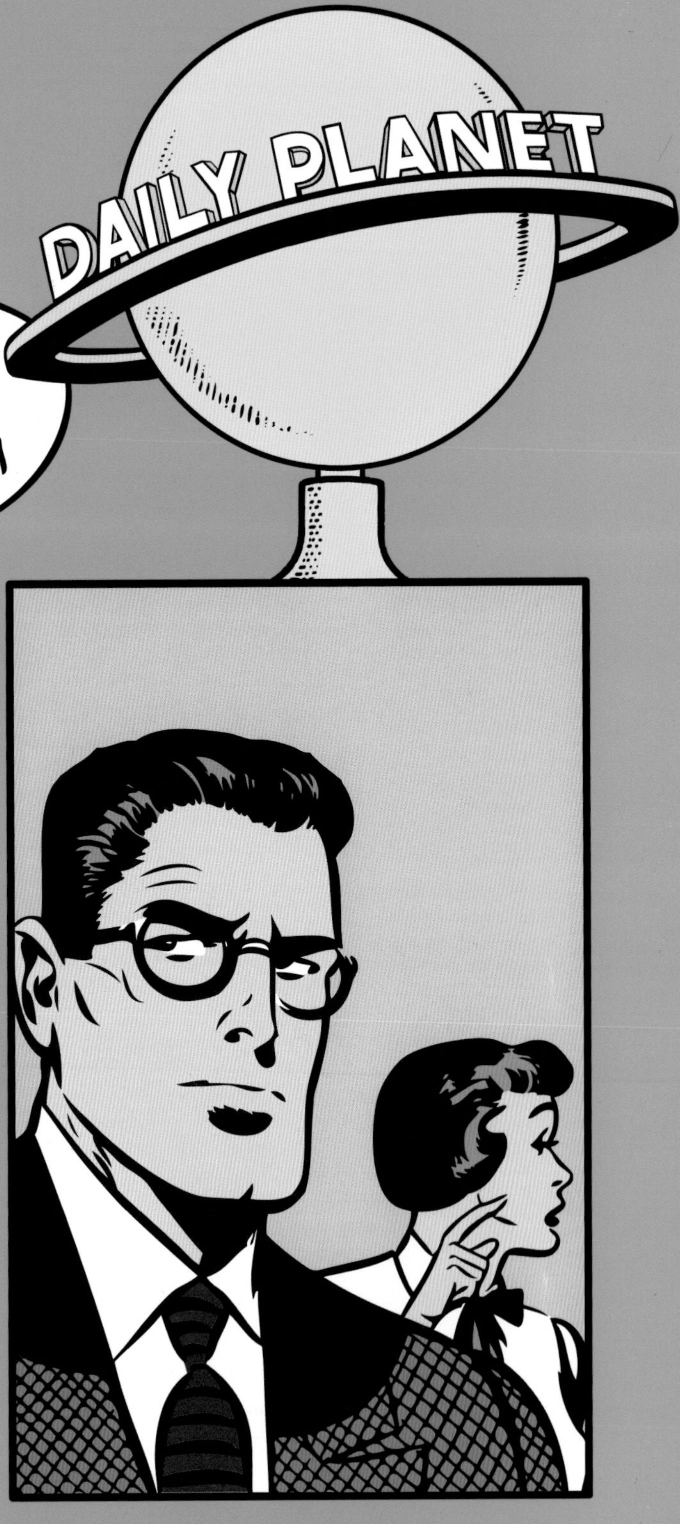
DAILY PLANET

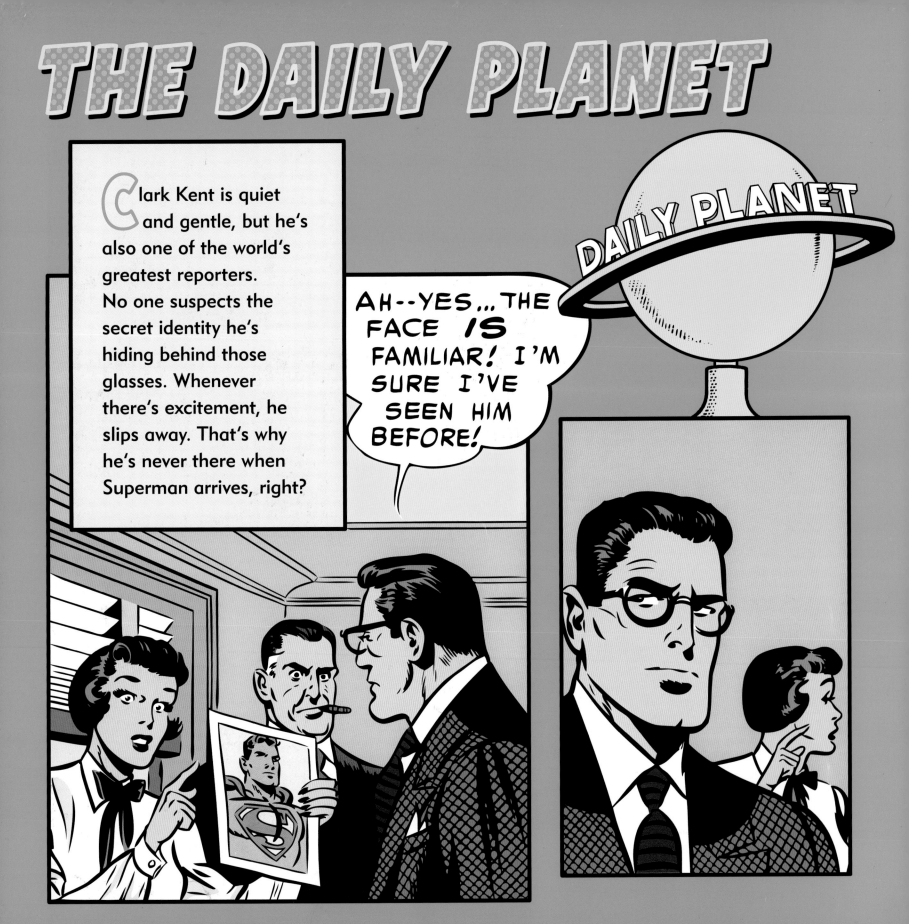

Clark works at the *Daily Planet* newspaper with Lois Lane and Jimmy Olsen. Their boss is the gruff but caring editor Perry White.

Lois Lane is smart, quick, and fearless when she chases down a story. If any reporter on Earth can match Clark Kent, it's her. Jimmy Olsen is young. He is still learning the newspaper business.

If Jimmy gets into trouble while investigating a story, he uses his signal watch to alert Superman. Jimmy gets in trouble a lot.

SOLAR-POWERED SUPERPOWERS

Under their own red sun, Kryptonians are just like human beings. Exposure to Earth's yellow sun gives Superman amazing powers: super-speed, flight, super-vision, super-hearing, super-strength, invulnerablity, and more.

Higher than any bird, and faster than any plane, Superman can soar through the sky, ready to swoop down on a criminal or catch a falling friend.

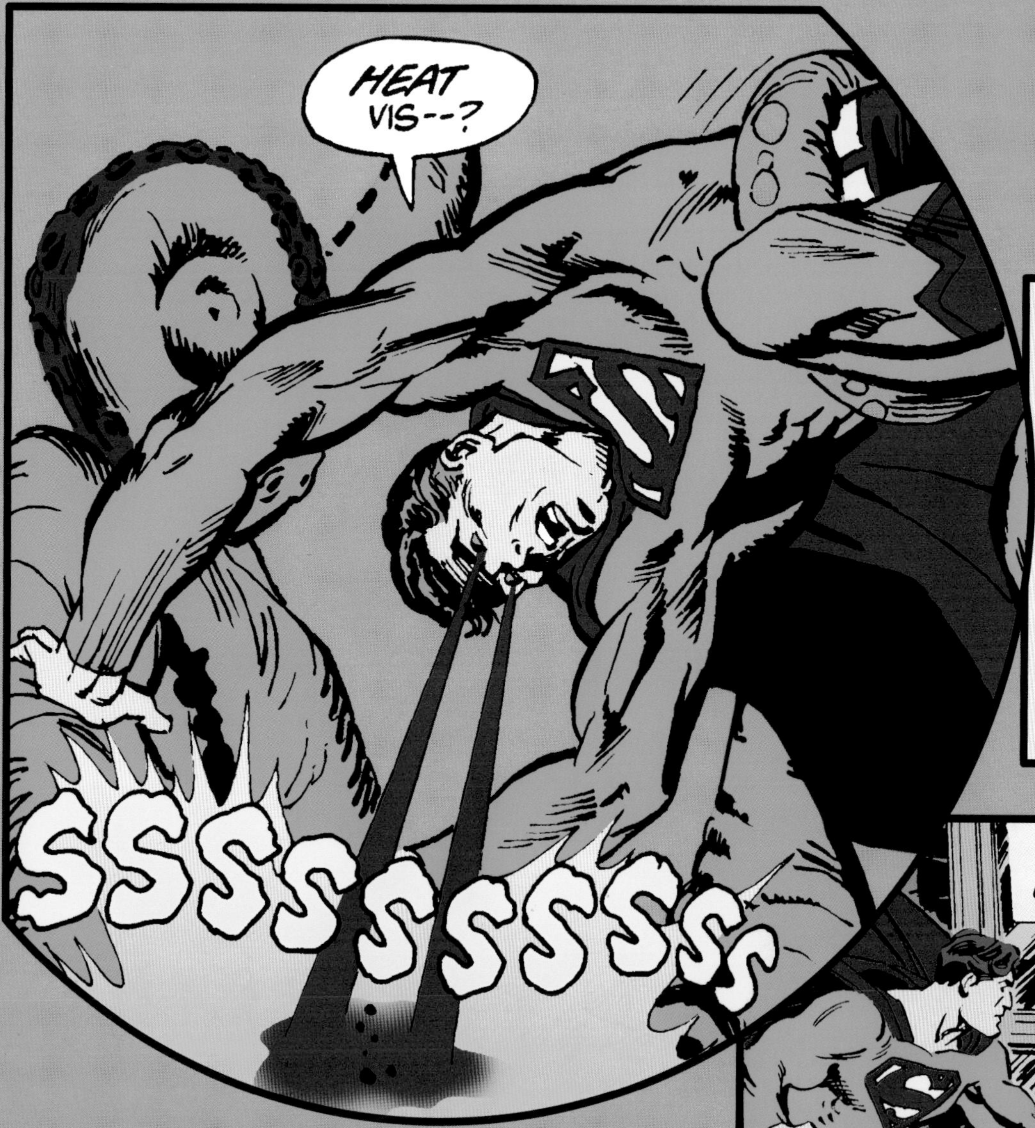
HEAT VIS--?
SSSSSSSSSS

Superman's heat vision can melt metal or even zap an out-of-control monster. With his X-ray vision, he can see through anything except lead.

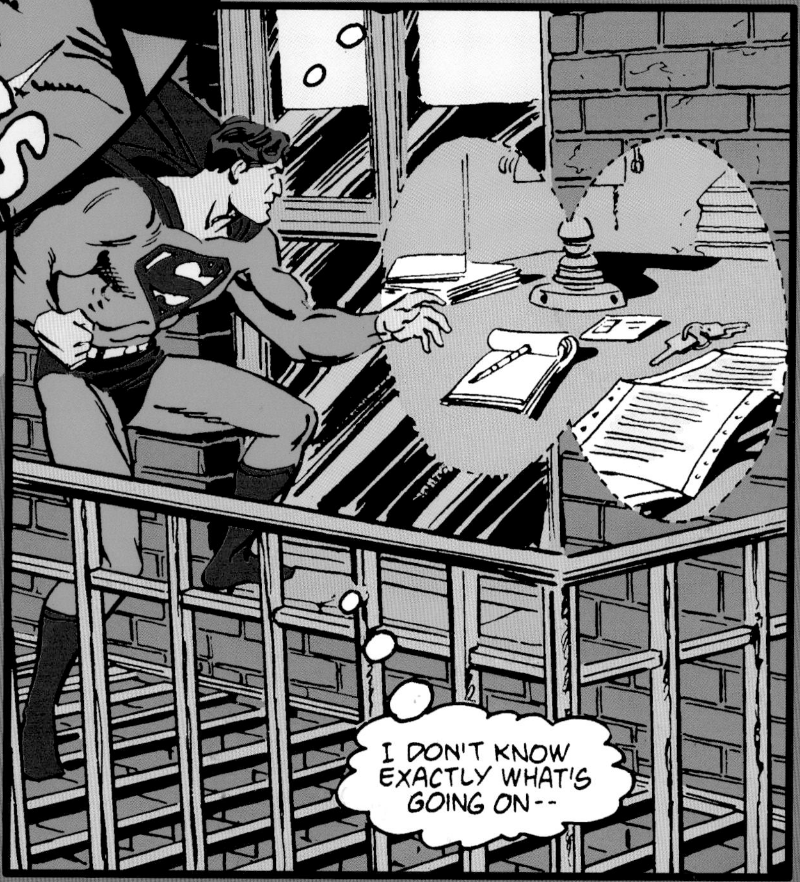
I DON'T KNOW EXACTLY WHAT'S GOING ON--

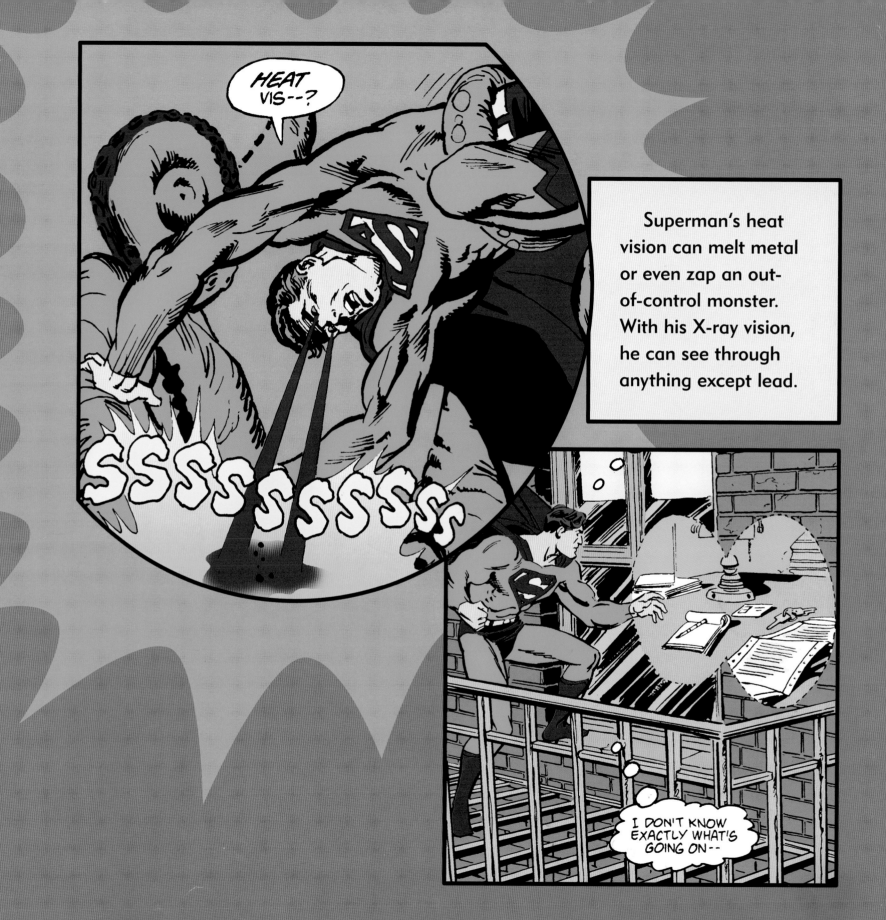

Superman can lift whole buildings into the air, smash walls, and rip through metal as easily as tissue paper.

There isn't much that can hurt Superman. Bullets bounce off his chest! Bombs can't scratch him! Superman can survive in outer space or fly right through the heart of a star, without even getting a sunburn.

Superman can punch through a streaking comet!

KRYPTONITE-MARE!

Superman can't be hurt by bullets, blades, fire, explosions, or other hazards. So what slows down the Man of Steel? Superman's greatest weakness is Kryptonite. When Krypton exploded, chunks of the planet blew all across the universe. These pieces took on unusual qualities. The most common kind of Kryptonite is green. It can cause Superman great pain and drain him of his powers. If he were exposed to it for long enough, it could even kill him.

GOSH, *BATMAN*, IS THAT THE *MIGHTY SUPERMAN*?

YES, *ROBIN*, BUT THEY'RE SPRAYING HIM WITH LIQUID *KRYPTONITE* THE ONLY SUBSTANCE THAT CAN DESTROY HIM! WE'VE GOT TO HELP HIM!

KRYPTONITE HANDBOOK!

GREEN K
CREATED BY THE RADIATION OF THE EXPLODING PLANET *KRYPTON*. EXPOSURE TO IT CAUSES *WEAKNESS* AND IS EVENTUALLY *FATAL*, BUT *ONLY* TO NATIVES OF KRYPTON.

RED K
THE RESULT OF METEOROIDS OF *GREEN K* PASSING THROUGH A *CRIMSON, COSMIC CLOUD*. EFFECTS ON KRYPTONIANS ARE *UNPREDICTABLE* AND *TEMPORARY*.

GOLD K
THEORY SUGGESTS *GOLD K* IS PRODUCED BY EXPOSING *GREEN K* OR *RED K* TO INTENSE NUCLEAR RADIATION. IT WILL PERMANENTLY ROB KRYPTONIANS OF THEIR *SUPER-POWERS*.

BLUE K
AN IMPERFECT DUPLICATION OF *GREEN K* MANUFACTURED BY SUPERMAN USING PROF. DALTON'S "DUPLICATOR RAY" MACHINE. HARMLESS TO KRYPTONIANS, BUT DEADLY TO *SUPER BIZARROS*.

WHITE K
FORMED WHEN *GREEN K* METEOROIDS PASSED THROUGH A *SPACE CLOUD*. DEADLY ONLY TO *PLANT LIFE*, OF ANY WORLD.

CITY SAVIOR

From the gleaming skyscrapers of downtown to the colorful docks of Metropolis Bay, Superman's city bustles with millions of people at work, school, or play. Seeing Superman makes the people of Metropolis feel safe. It also reminds them that power can be used for good and encourages them to do good in the world too.

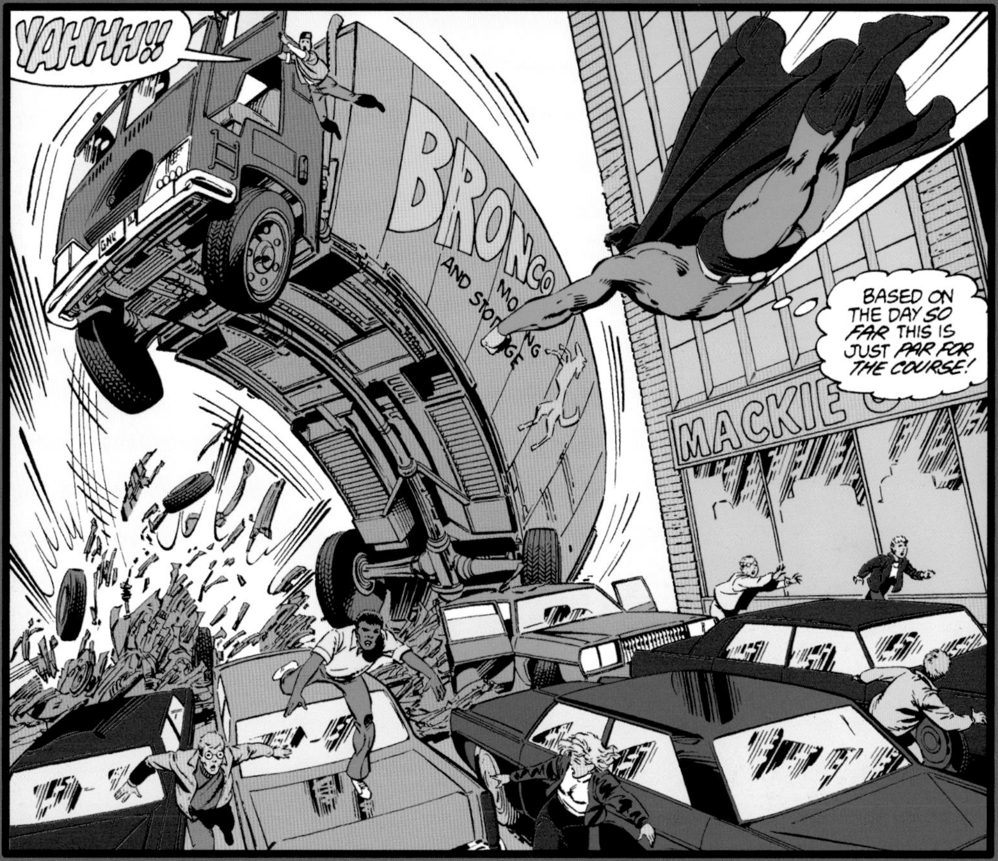
YAHHH!!
BRONCO
MACKIE
BASED ON THE DAY SO FAR THIS IS JUST PAR FOR THE COURSE!

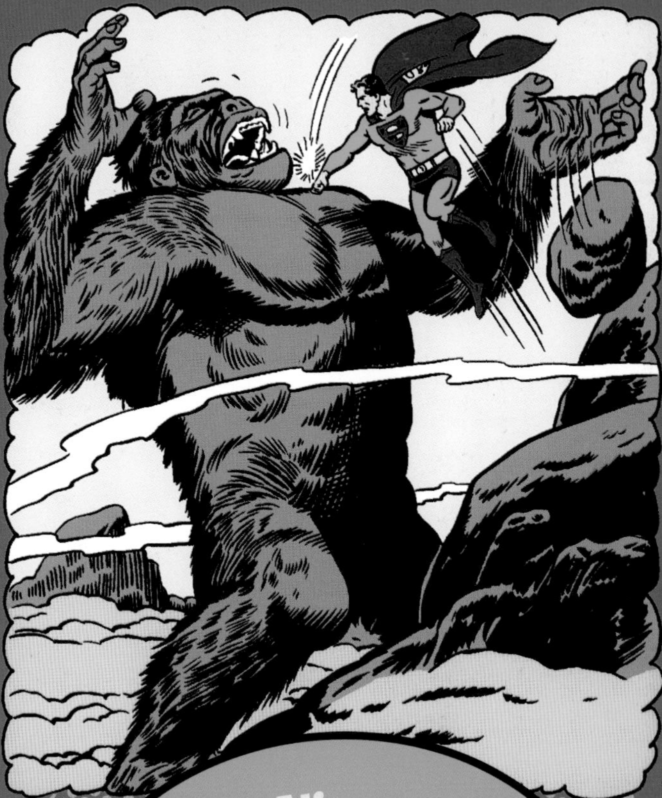

Alien invasions? Giant apes? Evil robots? Superman has saved Metropolis from them all!

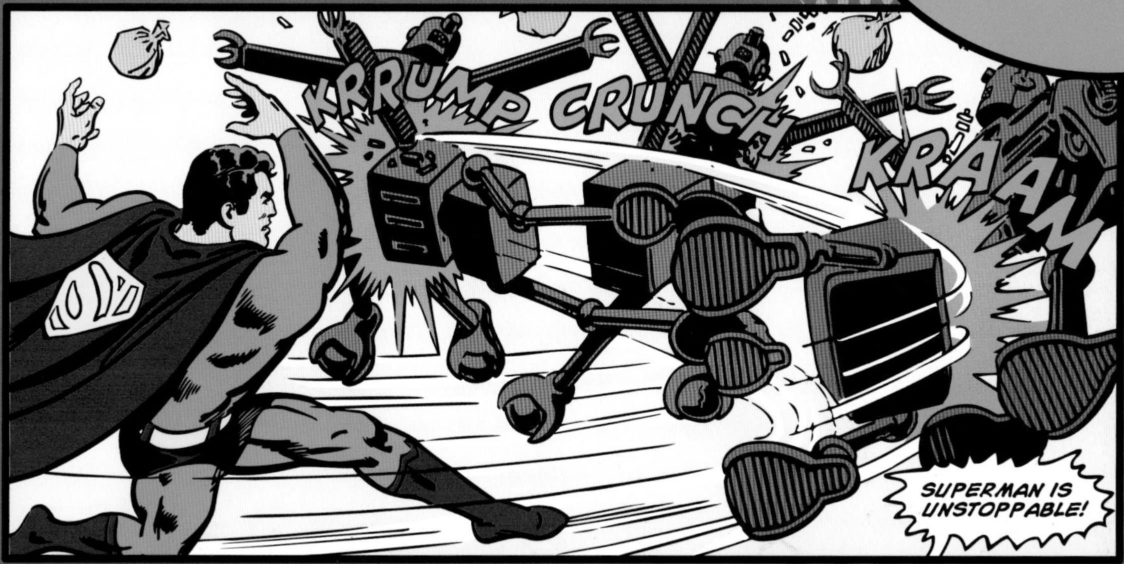
KRRUMP
CRUNCH
KRAAM
SUPERMAN IS UNSTOPPABLE!

Even super heroes need a little alone time every now and then. That's why Superman built his Fortress of Solitude in the frozen tundra near the North Pole.

Inside, Superman keeps mementos of his adventures, statues of his friends, and a memorial to Krypton.

Only Superman can lift the giant key to open the door of the Fortress of Solitude.

FORT SUPERMA

Villains would love to discover Superman's home away from home, so it must remain a secret. Only Batman, Supergirl, Lois Lane, and a few of Superman's other close friends have ever visited. One guest who's always welcome is Superman's four-legged friend Krypto!

When Kal-El's puppy landed on Earth from Krypton, he got superpowers too. Krypto is the Dog of Steel!

SUPERMAN'S MENACES

Superman has stopped all kinds of foes, from common crooks to alien invaders.

LEX LUTHOR

This power-hungry billionaire is jealous of Superman. He wants to crush him and rule Earth his own selfish way.

GOT SOME *THINGS* HERE THAT I THINK BELONG TO *YOU,* LUTHOR.

NUMBER *ONE,* YOUR KLAASH *ACTION TOY...*

GENERAL ZOD

This Kryptonian criminal was sent to a prison dimension called the Phantom Zone. But sometimes he escapes and appears on Earth to challenge Superman.

BRAINIAC

The evil mind of the alien robot Brainiac is faster and smarter than any computer.

DARKSEID

Darkseid controls the planet Apokolips. But he wants to control the entire universe. He is the strongest, nastiest villain around.

MR. MXYZPTLK

This imp from the Fifth Dimension loves to annoy Superman with his magical mischief. If Superman can trick him into saying his name backward, he'll be banished back home.

Can you say MXYZPTLK?
Forward= Miks-yez-pittle-ik
Backward= Kil-tipsy-zim

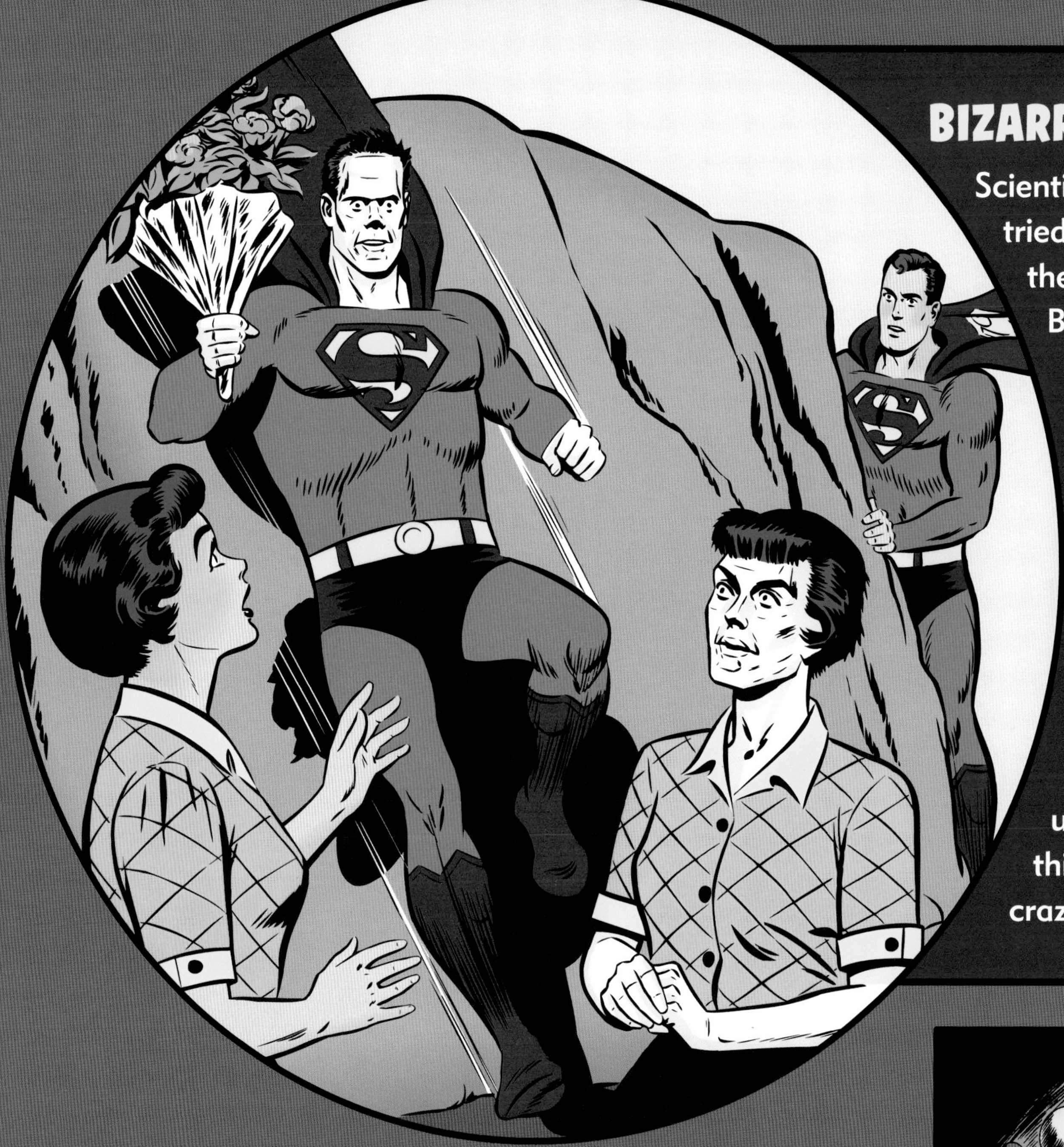

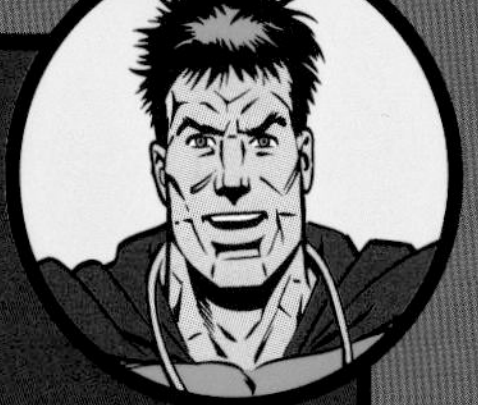

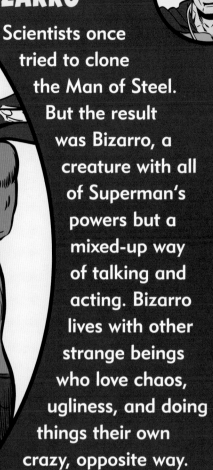

BIZARRO

Scientists once tried to clone the Man of Steel. But the result was Bizarro, a creature with all of Superman's powers but a mixed-up way of talking and acting. Bizarro lives with other strange beings who love chaos, ugliness, and doing things their own crazy, opposite way.

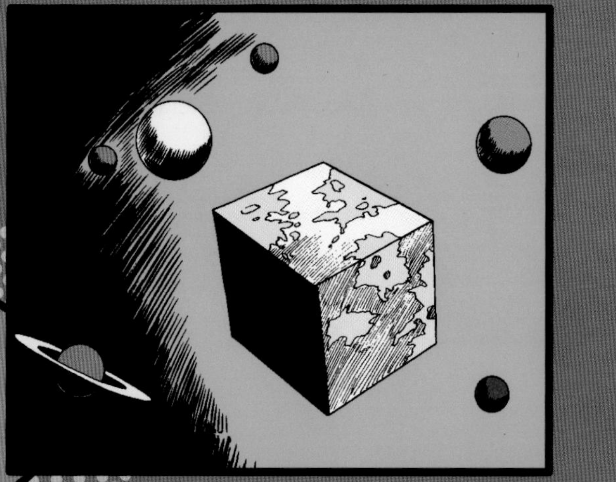

Bizarro's home planet isn't round. It's shaped like a cube!

SUPERMAN'S FRIENDS

Superman has many allies in his battle for justice. When he teams up with these heroes, they're unstoppable!

BATMAN

Batman's detective skills have helped Superman crack countless cases. The Dark Knight and the Man of Steel have different methods but common goals.

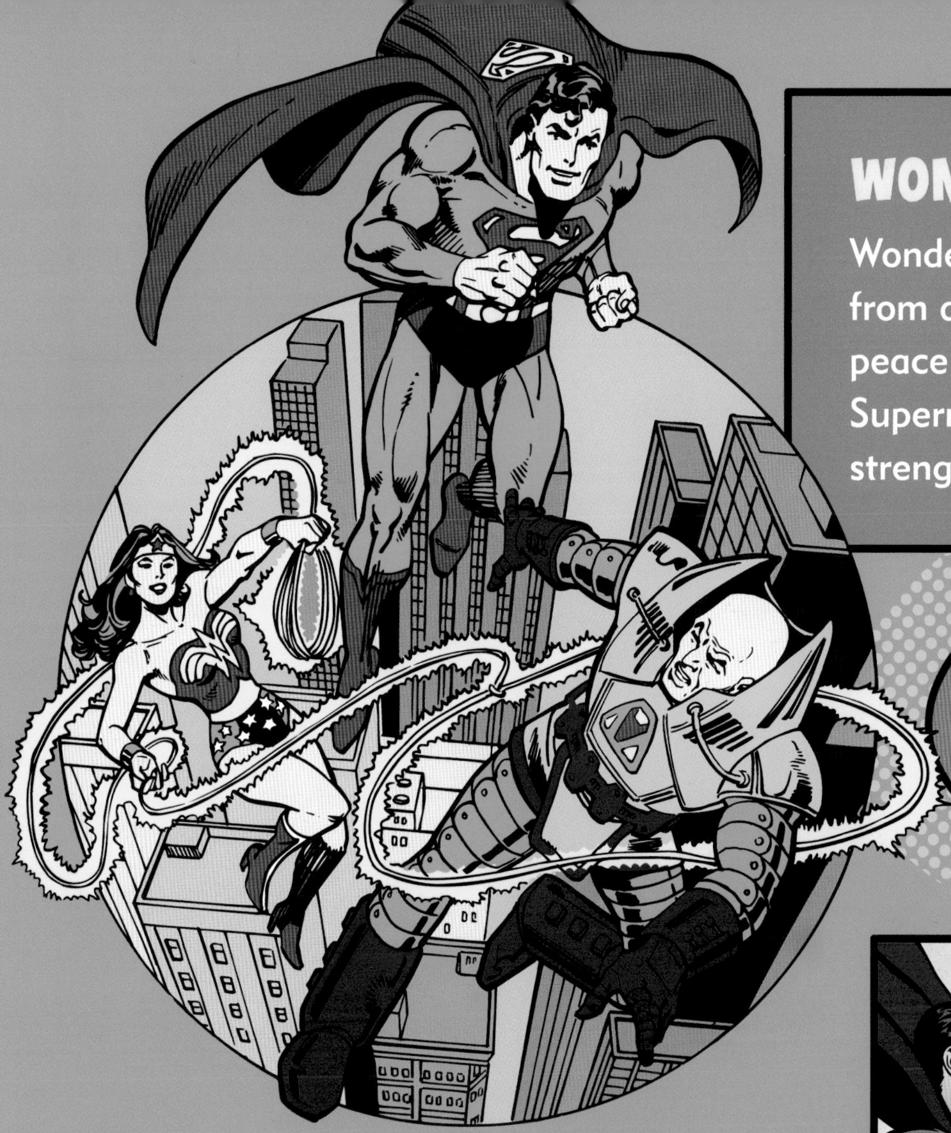

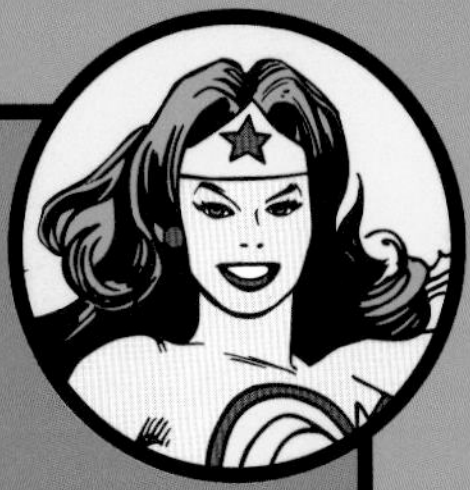

WONDER WOMAN

Wonder Woman also came from a distant place to fight for peace and good in the world. Like Superman, she is gifted with great strength, speed, and fighting skills.

Superman and Wonder Woman both use their powers to help everyone, everywhere.

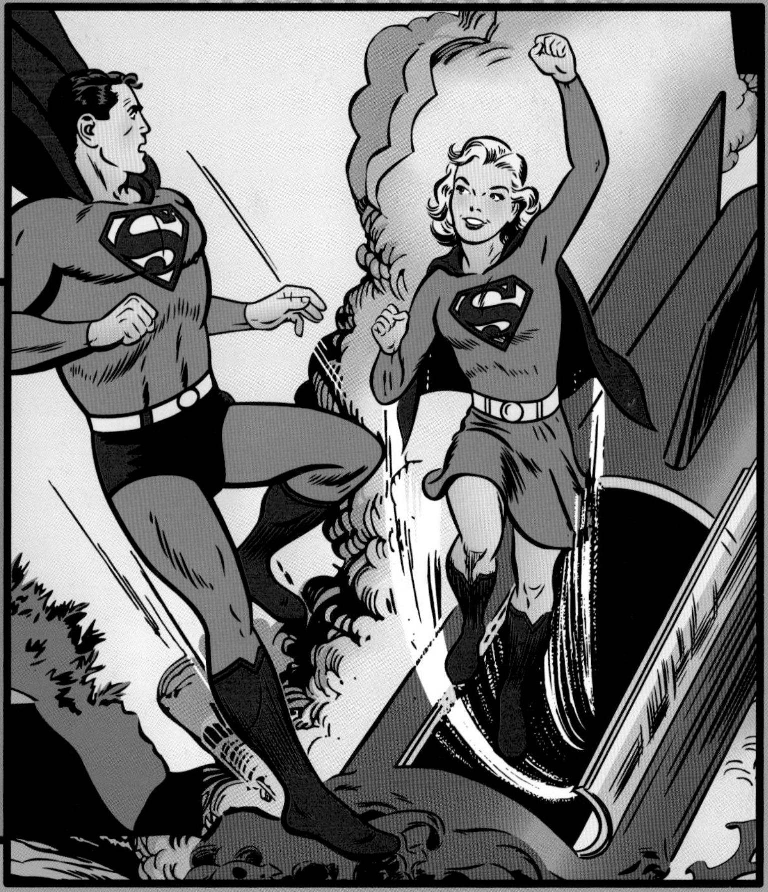

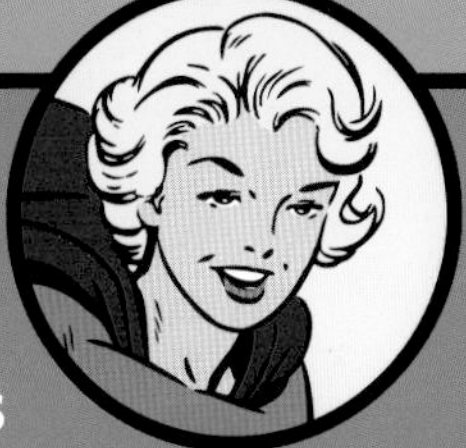

SUPERGIRL

Kara Zor-El is Superman's cousin. She too left Krypton as a child, but she didn't arrive on Earth until she was a teenager. Superman introduced her to her new home and helped her master her powers.

BIG-LEAGUE HEROES

Superman, Batman, and Wonder Woman are proud members of the Justice League of America, a team of Earth's greatest protectors. Members come from across the globe, beneath the seven seas, and even other planets.

JUSTICE LEAGUE of AMERICA

The members of the Justice League bring their own skills and powers to the team. With Green Lantern's power, Cyborg's bionic brain, Supergirl's strength, Green Arrow's awesome archery, and more, the Justice League is the ultimate force for good.

Superman is always trying to help people and make the world a better place. What would you do with superpowers? Would you fly to the moon? Use your X-ray vision to find buried treasure? Would you help people too?